HiT entertainment

First published in Great Britain 2011 by Dean
an imprint of Egmont UK Limited
239 Kensington High Street,
London W8 6SA

All rights reserved
ISBN 978 0 6035 6606 6
1 3 5 7 9 10 8 6 4 2
Printed in Malaysia

Mother's Helper

It was a busy day in Pontypandy. Helen Flood was going away for a few days, leaving her husband, Mike, to look after the house. Before she left, they went to pick up some groceries.

Naughty Norman was helping his mam, Dilys, in the supermarket, when he overheard them talking about the household chores.

"How am I going to manage all the chores?" Mike said, with a worried look on his face. "What will I do if someone needs a plumber?"

"It's OK, Mike, Mandy will help," Helen reassured him. "Norman helps out, doesn't he, Dilys?"

"No! Not Norman! I do all the housework myself — I wish he would help!" Dilys said.

Norman, alarmed at the mention of chores, saw his opportunity to escape. He sneaked around the end of a shopping aisle making a speedy getaway.

Meanwhile, at the Fire Station, it was also chore day. Elvis was mopping the floor upstairs, singing as he worked. Fireman Sam was busy cleaning Jupiter in the garage downstairs.

"Watch out, Penny. The floor is wet!" Elvis warned, just as he skidded in a puddle of water and fell into the fire pole hole, landing right on top of Sam!

A shocked Sam and Elvis both got up and dusted themselves off.

"Is everything OK down there?" Penny asked.

"Yes, Penny! Nothing broken - except Elvis' mop!" Sam replied.

Back in the village shop, Dilys was trying to get Norman to help with the housework. Norman wanted to go skateboarding and was just getting in her way.

"Norman Price! I have a job for you!" Dilys called out.

Just as Norman was trying to escape, he ran straight into Bronwyn.

"Not so fast, young man! Today, you are mother's little helper! Now, how can I help you, Bronwyn?" Dilys asked, as Norman sloped back into the supermarket.

At the Flood's house, Helen handed her husband a piece of paper through the ambulance window, and drove off. Mike and Mandy waved goodbye to Helen.

Mike unfolded the paper and looked at Mandy. It was a list of jobs he needed to remember.

"Don't worry, Dad. I'll look after you," Mandy said.

Mike was worried, the list of jobs was **VERY** long!

Back in the supermarket, Norman was upstairs in his room. His mam told him to pick up his dirty clothes and put them in the laundry basket.

"When you are finished, you can take the basket down to the cellar and put on a wash!" Dilys called back upstairs to Norman.

Norman had other plans. He would do the job as quickly as possible and then go skateboarding with Mandy.

That would be much more fun, he thought, as he crammed the dirty clothes into the washing machine. Norman then poured a generous helping of soap into the drawer.

He pushed the door shut and pressed the button. There was the sound of running water.

"There we go, I'm free!" Norman said, as he went to find his skateboard.

At the Floods' house, Mike and Mandy were working their way through Helen's list of chores. Mike was just about to get started on the ironing when Mandy came downstairs.

"I've tidied my room, made my bed and washed all of the dishes – my chores are done!" said Mandy to her dad, looking very pleased with herself.

"Great, you can help me with the ironing," Mike replied.

"No, thanks! I'm meeting Norman in the village, we're going skateboarding," Mandy said, as she ran for the door.

At the supermarket, Elvis was looking for a new mop.

"SHHHHHH! Can you hear that, Elvis?" Dilys said.

They both listened hard. There was the sound of running water.

"The washing machine!" screeched Dilys. There was water all over the cellar floor!

"Quick, Dilys, call Mike Flood the plumber – it's an emergency!" Elvis cried.

Mike was still busy with the ironing when he picked up Dilys' call.

"Say no more, Dilys. I'm on my way!" he said.

Mike set the iron down, hung up the phone and rushed to the rescue.

Mike looked at the washing machine as Dilys mopped up the water.

"You'll need a new part," Mike said. "You must have overloaded it."

"It was Norman Price! I won't ask him to do anything again!" Dilys replied.

Mike laughed and took his tools upstairs.

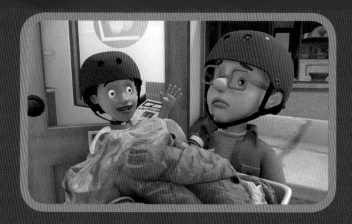

Just then, Norman and Mandy came into the supermarket.

"What now?! I did the washing!" said Norman, looking annoyed.

"You broke the washing machine! So you will need to use Mike's," said Dilys, handing him the wet washing.

Mike and Mandy laughed, as Norman followed them out the door.

As Mike's van pulled up to his house, Norman smelt something strange. Mike let Norman in through the door.

"Oh no! The ironing board is on fire!!" cried Norman.

"Call Fireman Sam, immediately!" Mike cried, looking alarmed.

ACTION STATIONS!

"Fire at the Flood's house, Sam.
Penny, take Venus as well . . ."
cried Station Officer Steele.

It wasn't long before Fireman Sam
and Elvis were in Jupiter and on
their way. Penny followed in Venus.

When they arrived, everyone
was standing outside and the
fire was blazing.

"Come away from the house, Mike!"
ordered Fireman Sam. "We'll take it
from here. Elvis – turn
off the electricity!"

"Right, Sam!"
replied Elvis.

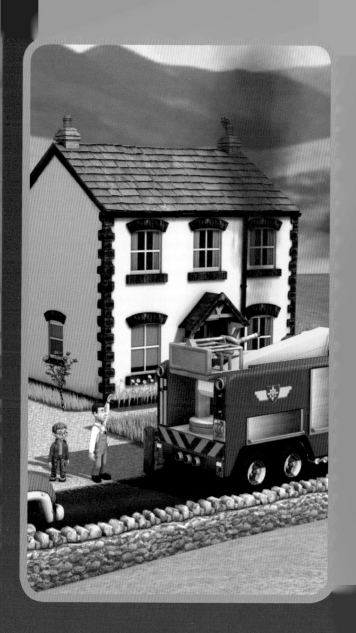

Fireman Sam and his crew put on their masks and got to work. Elvis used a fire extinguisher to put out the flames, and finally the fire was out.

Sam saw the pile of ironing that Helen had asked Mike to do. The iron was still on the ironing board – on top of a shirt. It must have caused the fire.

Together, Sam and his crew had saved the day!

Sam and Elvis came out of the house. Mike hung his head in shame.

"It's all my fault. I was hurrying to help Dilys and I must have left the iron on," Mike said, still looking at his feet.

"Well, we could all be a little more careful – whatever job we are doing!" Sam warned. "Right, Mike?"

"Yes, Sam," Mike replied.

"Right, Norman?" Mike continued.

"Yes, Mike," Norman answered.

"So, we've all learnt a lesson today then!" said Fireman Sam.

"Indeed!" Elvis laughed. "Even a mop can be dangerous!"